SID BISHOP

Witch Fate

Contents

1	Ashes	1
2	A New World	5
3	A Mind Recognized	8
4	The Orchard	14
5	Twilight	18
6	Conformity	23
7	The Fire Within	26
8	Broken	29
9	Resolve	31
10	A Knock at Dusk	33
11	The Heart Reclaimed	36
12	The Cost of Courage	40
13	Accused	43
14	The Promise	48
15	The Gallows	52
16	The Waiting Place	56
17	Fate	59
Afterword		60

1

Ashes

England, 1651

London was devouring itself in smoke and flame, and Katherine had run out of places to hide. She stood at the edge of the field, her cloak pulled tight around her shoulders, watching the fire crawl up the thatched roof of Mistress Bell's cottage. The orange light danced like it enjoyed the ruin. No one moved to help. Not the magistrate. Not the boys who used to buy herbs from Bell's cart. They all stood in silence, watching the blaze hollow the house to ash.

"They say it was an accident," someone whispered behind her.

But Katherine had seen the oil poured at the base of the wall. She had heard the quiet clicks of a shutter being fastened from the outside.

Her fingers trembled inside her sleeves, but she kept her chin high. She had learned long ago that trembling invited questions, and questions were dangerous for a girl who read Latin better than her brother and could name every herb in the woods behind her house.

Bell was gone. The fire had taken her, or someone had taken

her first and set the fire to erase it. And Katherine feared she would be next.

When the ashes cooled and the smoke turned from black to lazy gray, someone finally said,

"The fire took what it was told to take."

It was the same cold phrase they used when they buried her mother the year before. They said it while Katherine stood over a body that had been too thin, too quiet, too accused. A woman who knew too much about stars and salves. A woman who had taught Katherine to speak softly, but remember everything.

She had remembered.

And now she was alone.

Two weeks later, the boat was ready. And so was she.

That night, she packed her satchel and the leather-bound book her mother left her. She left without a goodbye.

The magistrate spoke quietly with the family who had taken her in. She was to leave England, passage arranged for the colonies across the sea. A new world, they called it. There was talk of tolerance there, of room enough for the curious and unwanted.

If England had no place for her, then perhaps America would. At least there, cleverness could be a tool instead of a curse.

"You'll make a wife of someone," the woman said to her flatly as she packed the bundle of wool and bone buttons. "Or you'll make trouble. Best you do it far from here."

Katherine didn't cry. Not when she kissed the stone wall of her mother's garden one last time. Not when she passed the tree where her father used to chart constellations by candlelight. Not even when the ship's deck cracked under her feet as she left the only place she'd ever known.

But that first night aboard the Providence, as the wind howled like wolves and the water churned dark as ink, she opened her mother's book.

It was small, bound in worn leather, and smelled like ash. Inside were pages of drawings, notes in cramped script, pressed herbs, moon phases, and strange symbols. Her mother had said it belonged to a woman before her, and another before that. Now it belonged to her.

Katherine read until her eyes burned. Then she pressed the book to her chest and whispered to the memory of her past.

The journey lasted seven weeks.

The crew grew uneasy around her. She wrote things in a book. She asked questions.

"Too clever by half," one sailor muttered.

"She speaks to the birds," another whispered.

The voyage was long and cruel, the sea tossing the ship like a child's toy. Katherine had grown used to the cold spray and the groans of weary passengers, but one evening she noticed the small boy huddled near the stern, shivering without a blanket.

She slipped off her own shawl, worn but warm, and draped it around his shoulders.

The boy blinked up at her, startled. "But then you'll be cold," he said.

Katherine crouched so they were eye level, a faint smile tugging at her mouth. "I've weathered worse," she told him. "Besides, you'll return it when we see land, won't you?"

He nodded solemnly, clutching the shawl tight.

As the ship creaked on into the night, Katherine sat beside him, humming a tune she half-remembered from childhood. She had no family here, no place to claim her, but at least for that moment, the boy leaned against her arm and slept in peace.

The next morning, he offered her a piece of dried apple and

told her his family had land in a place called Wethersfield. He had dark eyes and hands calloused like a man's.

"You can't read on the Sabbath," he warned gently. "They'll call it witching."

She smiled. "Then I'll read in the dark."

He looked at her strangely, but didn't press. And she liked that about him.

Land appeared like a ghost one morning, shrouded in mist. The captain shouted orders, and the crew scurried to life, but Katherine stood still, watching the gray shore of Connecticut rise before her like a cold promise.

As they docked, Samuel nudged her shoulder. "This is it. A place where anything can happen."

Katherine nodded. She would keep her mother's book hidden, her eyes open, and her heart quiet. For now.

She stepped onto the dock, felt the cold bite of New England wind against her cheeks, and took her first breath in the colony.

It tasted like wood smoke, salt and hope.

2

A New World

The sails flapped like the wings of a dying bird as she crossed the dock. Fog clung to the edges of the shore like it was hiding something, and maybe it was. A few children stood barefoot on the rocks, watching the ship with solemn eyes. Behind them, a cluster of women, bonnets tight, hands clasped.

She stood tall at the bow, her black cloak trailing in the morning wind, raven hair unbound and damp. Her eyes, dark and still, swept across the shoreline with observation.

To them, she looked like an omen.

"She's not dressed like a servant," one woman hissed.

"She stands like a man," another muttered.

"She watches too closely."

Katherine stepped off the gangplank and felt the brittle earth of the new world beneath her boots for the first time. It felt nothing like England. The place smelled of pine smoke and sweat, and there was a sharpness to the air she couldn't quite name.

Samuel stood beside her, clutching his hat like a boy at church. "This is home."

Katherine didn't answer. The fog had thinned just enough to reveal crooked houses and muddy roads. Everything was wooden, crude, temporary, like the town was waiting for someone to decide if it deserved to survive.

As they passed the townspeople, she heard their whispers. They didn't bother hiding them.

"She doesn't lower her gaze."

"Where is her family?"

"A woman alone is a danger."

"No husband, no chaperon, no shame."

The men didn't speak, but they looked. First at her face, then her figure. Then, too long, at the book strapped to her belt.

One man spat into the dirt.

Samuel tried to keep pace, but even he seemed smaller beside her now. "They'll get used to you," he said, not sounding convinced.

She was taken in by a widowed family in Wethersfield who "owed a favor" to the magistrate. A barn loft was offered, cold and dry, with straw enough to sleep on and a cracked window that looked out at the forest edge. When she unrolled her few belongings, her book, her mother's ring, the herb pouch Samuel had given her, the woman of the house narrowed her eyes.

"Women here sew, cook, bear children," she said flatly. "They do not read. Especially not from… strange books."

Katherine met her gaze. "Then perhaps I'll only read when no one's looking."

The woman made a sound between a scoff and a curse and left her to settle in silence.

That night, Katherine walked beyond the fields to the edge of the woods. The moon hung low, thick and red like blood behind clouds. She reached into her cloak and withdrew the book. She knelt and traced the ground with her fingers. The soil here was dry, stubborn.

Behind her, back at the house, a shutter banged against the wall. The baby cried. The woman muttered that the air had gone strange.

By the end of her first week, the rumors had already begun.

"The child's fever worsened after she passed the gate."

"She keeps herbs no one recognizes."

"I saw her talking to a blackbird. And it talked back."

Katherine made no effort to correct them. What was the point?

She walked through the town like a shadow in daylight, silent, watchful, always one step removed. She didn't lower her eyes when men stared or when women turned their backs. She read by candlelight, never on Sundays. She stitched her own seams, boiled her own broth, and greeted each day with the quiet resolve to build something steady from the pieces she'd been given.

3

A Mind Recognized

It was market day when Katherine first saw him.

The square hummed with life. Children darted between stalls, women bartered loudly over salted fish and wool, and the scent of baked bread curled through the breeze. It was the first warm morning in weeks, and the entire town seemed to exhale into the sun. Katherine lingered near the well. Her eyes traced movements, habits, exchanges. She found patterns in people the way others found them in the stars.

Then came the horses, sleek, polished, out of place. They trotted into the square with just enough noise to turn heads.

At the center of the group sat a man in a dark blue coat, worn at the edges but clearly fine once. He was older than the local boys, younger than the ministers, with sharp features and eyes like storm light. He dismounted with a fluid grace, boots hitting the ground as if the earth welcomed him back.

The crowd stirred.

"Governor Winthrop," someone whispered.

Katherine blinked. That was the governor?

She had expected something pompous. Colder. Instead, he

looked amused by the entire world.

Winthrop greeted the blacksmith with a clap on the back, asked after a sick child by name, then took a moment to examine a hunk of quartz from the apothecary's table.

"Not bad," he said, flipping it in his hand. "But you've been sold fool's gold. Again."

The apothecary laughed nervously. "Still looks impressive in the window."

Winthrop smiled. "So do a lot of things."

When his gaze swept across the market, it landed unmistakably on Katherine.

He didn't look away. Didn't glance, didn't frown.

He watched.

So did she.

After a moment, he crossed the square, boots crunching in the gravel, and stopped two feet from her.

"You're new," he said.

"You're not," she replied.

A grin twitched at his mouth. "And clever. Excellent."

Katherine said nothing.

"I'm John Winthrop," he offered, as though she didn't already know. "I govern, sometimes. But mostly I'm just a glorified diplomat with a fascination for rocks and rude people."

She raised an eyebrow. "You're quite good at introductions."

"And you're quite good at not giving yours."

Katherine let the silence sit before answering. "Katherine Branch."

He nodded as if confirming a theory. "Branch. You read?"

She hesitated. "Yes."

"Write?"

"Yes."

"Latin?"

"…yes."

His smile widened. "A woman after my own inclinations. Though I find Greek a better teacher when one is looking for difficult truths."

Katherine almost smiled. Almost. "I find truth rarely cares for language."

Winthrop gave a sharp, delighted laugh. A few townspeople looked over, puzzled.

"Miss Branch," he said, his voice lowering slightly, "do be careful."

"Of what?" she asked.

"Of being interesting. This colony doesn't take kindly to it."

The encounter lasted only minutes, but it stayed with her like a melody she couldn't quite shake.

But she remembered how he had looked at her. Not with fear. Not with pity. Not like a man watching a woman.

Like a mind recognizing another.

As the market swelled again, and the governor moved on, a voice beside her said, "Well. That was dramatic."

Katherine turned.

A woman leaned against the well, arms folded, eyebrows lifted in amusement. She wore her bonnet pushed slightly too far back, dark curls peeking rebelliously at her temples. Her sleeves were dusted with flour and she smelled faintly of soap root and sassafras.

"Excuse me?" Katherine asked, uncertain whether to be defensive or intrigued.

"You're either incredibly brave," the woman said, "or entirely unaware that half the village already thinks you're cursed. Holding court with Governor Winthrop in full daylight? Bold."

Katherine narrowed her eyes. "And you are?"

"Elizabeth Seager," she replied with a mischievous half-curtsy. "Resident midwife. Reluctant laundress. Occasional scapegoat. And you, Miss Branch, are currently the most interesting thing to happen to Wethersfield since someone's goat gave birth to twins in the parlor."

Katherine blinked, then gave the smallest of smiles. "Good to know I've dethroned the goat."

"Just barely," Elizabeth said. "You'll need to work harder."

They stood in comfortable silence for a beat, watching the bustle swirl back around them.

"I'm not looking for attention," Katherine said eventually.

"Of course not," Elizabeth replied lightly. "Neither are thunderstorms. But people always seem to notice."

That pulled a genuine laugh from Katherine, short, surprised, and sharp.

Elizabeth gave her a sly look. "Careful. They'll accuse us both of sorcery for laughing in public."

"Let them," Katherine said, her tone dry.

Elizabeth smirked, brushing flour from her sleeves as she leaned against the edge of the apothecary stall. "You're not from here, that much is obvious."

Katherine's brow arched. "Is it my accent, or the fact that I'm not spitting into the wind about someone's salted pork?"

"Neither," Elizabeth said, inspecting her own fingernails. "It's the way you watch everything like it's a test you've already passed."

Katherine glanced up as a flock of starlings cut across the sky, their wings catching the light like sparks.

"You like birds?" she asked, surprised to see Elizabeth watching them too.

Elizabeth's eyes twinkled. "If I had wings, I'd never touch the ground again."

They stood in silence for a beat, the hum of the market filling the spaces between them. Then Katherine leaned a little closer.

"Is it always like this?"

"Market day? Or Wethersfield in general?"

Katherine tilted her head. "Both."

Elizabeth's grin softened. "Market days are noisy, but predictable. Wethersfield, though… it's quieter than it should be. Too many ears. Not enough mouths."

"And the women?"

"They'll size you up before they say hello. If they say hello."

"And the men?"

Elizabeth shrugged. "Useful if you need a roof raised or a fire started. Less useful if you need a conversation."

Katherine chuckled under her breath. "I'll keep that in mind."

A moment passed, and then she asked, more earnestly, "How do you stand it? The watching. The quiet judgment. I thought this was a place of tolerance."

Elizabeth didn't answer right away. Instead, she looked out across the square, where two matrons had paused their bartering to cast suspicious glances their way.

"It's certainly more tolerant than Europe. But that's not saying much. I stand it by pretending I don't notice," she said finally. "And when that fails… I bake."

"Bake?"

"Muffins mostly. People talk less when their mouths are full."

Katherine laughed. "Sound advice."

Elizabeth turned to her, voice dropping slightly. "Don't give them what they're looking for, Katherine. That's how they win. Act like you're just clever enough to be useful, but never clever enough to threaten. And for God's sake, never correct the minister."

"Even if he butchers the Latin?"

"Especially then."

Katherine shook her head, a smile tugging at her mouth despite herself.

"I like you," she said.

"Give it time," Elizabeth replied, dusting off her hands. "Most don't."

Both chuckled.

"Come find me sometime. I brew decent tea and tell better stories."

And just like that, she vanished into the crowd, leaving behind the faintest echo of mirth.

For the first time since arriving in Connecticut, Katherine felt something stir in her chest that wasn't dread.

It was the start of something. It felt...right.

4

The Orchard

The orchard sat quiet under a thin veil of morning fog, dew clinging to the grass like tiny beads of glass. Katherine wandered just beyond the split-rail fence, basket in hand, the soft rustle of leaves above her. She wasn't supposed to be this far from the market path, but the apples were better here, less picked over, less bruised by careless hands.

She had bent to pick one that had fallen outside the orchard fence. A perfect crimson sphere, still unbruised, when a voice behind her said, "Careful. That one's claimed."

She turned, straightening slowly, apple in hand. The man before her was older than most in Wethersfield, with gray threaded through his beard and lines at the corners of his eyes. He didn't look at her like the others did. Not with suspicion. Not with fear. Just quiet amusement.

"I didn't see a name on it," Katherine replied, her voice softer than usual.

She held out the apple. He made no move to take it.

"Keep it," he said. "It suits you."

"I'm John Harrison."

"Katherine Branch," she answered, hesitating just a little, a faint warmth stirring in her chest.

Katherine studied him for a beat longer. He didn't flinch under her gaze, didn't shift his weight like he wanted to leave. He simply waited, patient, like someone accustomed to silence and in no hurry to fill it.

She blinked. "What do you do, Mr. Harrison?"

"Fix what's broken. Read when I can. Plant trees that won't bear fruit until after I'm gone."

A smile tugged at the corner of her mouth, reluctant but real. "And collect fallen apples."

Another pause passed between them, easy this time.

"You should try the ones higher up," he said, gesturing toward the tree branches. "Sweeter than anything you'll find on the ground."

Katherine glanced up. "That's good advice."

"I'm full of it."

"I'll bet."

They parted without ceremony, but something lingered.

John lived on the edge of the settlement, with a modest house and a wide, clean field that caught the morning light. He was a widower. No children. No fuss. Kept to himself, read books, and had once taught Latin to the minister's son before they decided it was dangerous for boys to think too freely.

It wasn't long before she saw him again.

He came by the market stand where she traded herbs, offering too much coin for dried sage and a pinch of lemon balm.

"You could grow your own," she said.

"I could," he agreed. "But then I'd have no reason to come talk to you."

She blinked, a quiet laugh escaping her lips.

That winter was gentler than the last, and Katherine found herself looking forward to John's visits more often than she expected. When he walked with her to the riverbank one afternoon, she felt a flutter she hadn't felt in years, and an unexpected lightness in her chest.

They talked about books. And healing plants. And why crows remember faces.

John asked questions, real ones. Not to test her. Not to trap her. Just to understand.

For the first time in a long while, Katherine felt seen, not as a threat, not as a mystery, but as a person.

She didn't fall in love like in stories, with flushed cheeks and whispered declarations. But she fell into it, slowly, like dusk folding into night.

They married in the spring.

There was no big ceremony. Just a few witnesses, a walk through the orchard in uncharacteristic but stunning, off-white dress, and a simple gold ring slipped onto her hand beneath the apple trees.

Some said he was bewitched.

Others said he was lonely.

Neither seemed to bother him.

He brought her books and copper pots. She brought him warmth and conversation and long silences that felt companionable instead of cold.

She cooked simply. He fixed things that broke. And for a while, for a good while, there was peace.

It was John who first called it "the book of fire."

She had taken it out only once in front of him, when his shoulder ached so badly he couldn't lift his ax. She laid herbs on the table, fingers moving in quiet ceremony, and opened the black leather cover.

He watched in silence as she turned its pages. Some inked in Latin, others marked with lines and symbols she did not explain.

When she was done, he flexed his shoulder. The pain was gone.

He didn't ask questions.

But he kissed her forehead and said softly, "You'll need to be careful with that."

She knew.

At night, he'd fall asleep with his hand resting against her back, and she would lie awake tracing constellations in the knot-work of the wooden ceiling, pretending they were stars no one else had named.

She didn't dream often. But when she did, she sometimes saw herself walking through fire and not burning.

5

Twilight

She had felt the first stirrings of her son one crisp morning, a fluttering that made her heart catch and her hand press instinctively against her stomach. Her belly grew steadily through spring and John had been her constant companion through it all. Katherine had pictured what her child's face might look like, the sound of his cry, the tiny grasp of his hand.

Elizabeth had also been by her side from the first labor pains. Calm and steady, Elizabeth's hands guided Katherine through each contraction, her voice low and confident, offering instructions, encouragement, and gentle reassurances. She moved around the room with practiced precision, checking blankets, warming water, and preparing for the moment when the world would be made anew.

When the day finally came, hours of labor passed under Elizabeth's watchful care. The room filled with the rhythmic sound of her guidance and John's quiet murmurs of love. And then, at last, a cry split the air. A voice small and defiant, asserting itself in the world. Benjamin had arrived, and with him came a wave of relief, awe, and a fierce, immediate love.

Elizabeth carefully handed the swaddled infant into Katherine's waiting arms. Katherine held him close, feeling the warmth of his new life against her chest, the rapid flutter of his pulse beneath her hand, the soft sighs of his breathing as he settled into the world. John bent forward to kiss her temple, eyes shining, and Elizabeth offered a small, satisfied nod.

Weeks had passed since that quiet, urgent day. The early haze of sleepless nights and tender anxieties had settled into a gentle rhythm, and the world outside seemed to bloom in step with Benjamin's growth.

The orchard smelled of blossoms and rain. Her baby boy, Benjamin, was asleep inside, wrapped snug in a wool blanket, his steady breathing like a quiet promise. John sat beside her under the budding apple trees, reading from a worn book of poetry, one finger marking his place even as he looked up and smiled at her.

Their life had fallen into rhythm, tender, thoughtful, and fulfilling. Katherine, once a stranger and a shadow, now found joy in the smallest moments: the crack of eggshells on cold mornings, John's hand brushing hers across the dinner table, the sound of Benjamin's giggles. She had not expected to be loved like this.

The market in Wethersfield bustled with its usual morning clamor, merchants calling out their wares and baskets clattering against wooden stalls. Katherine moved among them, searching for herbs and other small necessities, when a thought struck her: she hadn't seen Elizabeth Seager since Benjamin's birth. She had meant to bring the midwife a small gift, a bundle of dried chamomile and lavender, to thank her. Smiling at the memory of Elizabeth's steady hands and quiet encouragement, Katherine approached the stall where Elizabeth usually tended.

"Good morning," Katherine said to the woman behind it. "Is Elizabeth here today? I hoped to give her something for helping with… well, for my son's birth."

The woman's face went pale, her lips tightening as she leaned closer. "Elizabeth Seager?" she whispered, glancing around as if the words themselves might carry danger. "My dear, she was hanged in Hartford, only yesterday. Found guilty of witchcraft."

Katherine's hands froze around her basket, her pulse quickening. The herbs felt suddenly heavy in her palms, her chest tightening. "Seager…" she murmured, tasting the name as if speaking it aloud could make sense of the horror.

John reached for her hand, grounding her. As they made their way back through the narrow streets toward the cart that would take them home. He said nothing, letting her thoughts settle at their own pace, though his eyes mirrored concern.

Later that night, Katherine sat beside Benjamin's cradle, her hand resting lightly in the curls at his crown. He slept with one hand fisted near his cheek, his breath soft and steady, a tiny metronome of trust.

Katherine struggled to reconcile the news of the woman who had soothed her pain, who had cradled Benjamin moments after his first cry, was gone. Hanged. The thought felt impossible, like a story told about someone else. Her mind kept circling back to Elizabeth's steady hands, her confident voice, the glimmer of mischief in her eyes, and the cruel, incomprehensible weight of a world that could snatch her away so suddenly.

The thought lodged itself in Katherine's chest like a splinter she couldn't pull free.

She imagined the rope. The silence of the crowd. The sound her shoes might've made against the wood before it dropped away.

Katherine glanced down at Benjamin and smoothed a curl behind his ear.

She had a good life now. A son who reached for her with both hands. A husband who touched her gently and listened with his whole attention. A home tucked far enough from the center of Wethersfield that she could still breathe when the walls of the town began to press in.

But that night Elizabeth's fate rattled inside her like an old bone charm.

It could be me, she thought. It could still be me.

The next morning, she poured out her tinctures. Not the dangerous ones, just the strong ones. The ones that worked too well. The ones people whispered about when their pain vanished too fast. She scrubbed the hearth with salt and ash, wiped the soot from the jars with a rough cloth, and packed the black-covered book deep beneath linens in the root cellar.

A week after the news of Seager's hanging, Katherine moved through the rows in silence, pruning white-pink flowers with a gentle hand.

That was when she felt it.

A stillness.

Not silence, there were birds, but a pause in the rhythm of the world, like the trees themselves had tilted toward her. Listening.

She turned slowly.

At the edge of the path stood a little girl, maybe eight years old, with her hands clasped behind her back and her bonnet too large for her head.

"Are you the woman who talks to animals?" the girl asked.

Katherine blinked, caught between the chill on her skin and the warmth in the girl's voice.

"I speak to my son," she said gently, brushing a blossom from her sleeve. "And he roars like a bear. Does that count?"

The girl giggled and dashed off toward the fields, her apron flapping behind her.

But the question stayed.

And that night, the wind brought no sleep.

In her dreams, Katherine saw Elizabeth standing barefoot in a golden field. The wheat moved with a breeze, but Elizabeth didn't. Her arms were outstretched.

And then the wheat caught fire. Not a fire that burned, but one that transformed.

Elizabeth didn't flinch.

She looked directly at Katherine.

And smiled.

When Katherine woke, her chest ached.

John stirred beside her. "Bad dream?" he murmured, half-asleep.

"No," she whispered, staring at the beams above. "A warning."

6

Conformity

Katherine Harrison had never known the weight of fear like this. But the news of Elizabeth Seager had lodged in her bones.

Not as a lesson.

As a warning.

It had been over a month since she learned about what happened, yet it echoed in her thoughts with cruel persistence. A mother. A healer. Convicted. Hanged.

She found herself turning down requests from neighbors. A tincture for headaches? She gave them plain willow bark, nothing more. A salve for fever? No herbs with names they couldn't pronounce.

She wore paler colors, brown, gray, cream, saving her black shawl for colder mornings. She sat in the back row at town meetings.

It didn't feel like safety.

It felt like shrinking.

One afternoon, while hanging linens, Katherine caught herself watching the women across the field, wives with plain bonnets and down-turned eyes, their movements synchronized like the rhythm of a prayer.

She tried, just for a moment, to imagine herself among them. A life where she smiled only when spoken to. Cooked what she was told. Let John do the speaking in town.

Benjamin squealed from the porch. She looked up and saw his tiny hands reaching for the cat's tail. She rushed to scoop him up, pressing her lips to his hair, and breathed in the scent of apples and milk.

She wanted him safe.

But would he be safer if his mother didn't stand out?

That night, she told John, "I'm thinking of joining the sewing circle of women."

He looked up from his book, brow raised. "You don't sew."

"I can learn," she said.

He didn't argue. Just set his book aside and pulled her gently into his lap, brushing his fingers through her hair.

"You know who you are," he said. "Don't forget that."

But she said nothing.

Because part of her didn't know anymore.

In her dreams that week, Elizabeth Seager reappeared. This time not in a field of wheat, but kneeling before a fire, her face turned away.

When Katherine approached, Seager whispered, "Fear has never needed proof. Only a target."

Katherine woke, heart racing, sweat soaking her nightgown.

She rose before dawn and washed her face with cold water. Stared at her reflection in the basin's surface. Her dark eyes didn't look mysterious in the faint light. They looked tired. Doubtful.

But even in her fear, something inside her stirred. Not defiance, not yet, but a flicker.

Like the very thing she was trying to bury was pushing back, just a little, testing the soil.

It would grow in time.

But for now, Katherine Harrison tied her apron, kissed her son's forehead, and stepped out into a world that demanded conformity… or conviction.

7

The Fire Within

Spring arrived like a secret whispered across the orchard.

Benjamin, now a young boy, chased sunspots between the apple trees, his laughter echoing off the budding branches. His stride was sure, his voice strong, his questions endless. Katherine answered them all with a smile that felt practiced, though warm.

John watched them from the porch, his frame thinner than last year. The cough still came and went, sharp and dry like brittle leaves. He waved it off each time. She stopped pressing.

Life, on the surface, was good.

The town approved of her now. Her hair was tied neatly each morning. Her skirts plain. Her books shelved. She traded herbs but didn't speak of what they did. She answered questions with modesty and let others speak louder.

She laughed in the marketplace when expected. She nodded. She made broth for the sick and delivered it with eyes lowered.

And the town was pleased.

Since Winthrop had sailed for England to secure the charter, the elders grew more eager to prove their piety. Without his tempering presence, whispers of the Devil grew louder. A girl with a fever cried out in her sleep—witch. A goat miscarried—witch. A man stumbled drunk into a ditch—witch.

Elizabeth Seager's death had not satisfied their blood-lust. If anything, it had inflamed it.

Katherine felt it in the pause of conversations when she entered a room. In the way her name hung just behind people's teeth.

She kept her head down. Smiled more. Spoke less.

She hadn't opened the book in nearly a year. Hadn't touched it since Benjamin was small enough to cradle. Still, sometimes at night, she thought she heard it whisper beneath the linens where it lay hidden in the chest.

John's cough deepened that spring. He dismissed it, as always, with a joke or a shrug. But Katherine saw the shadows beneath his eyes, the way his hands trembled when he chopped wood, how long it took him to catch his breath.

The book of fire still tucked away, its leather worn and heavy, and she could feel its pull. Somewhere inside were the remedies, the secret cures, the knowledge that might save him. But opening the book, using it… that was a line she had promised herself she would not cross. To conform. To live quietly. To avoid suspicion.

And yet the thought of John, his fever climbing, his body wasting, tore at her resolve. She imagined the worst: him slipping away, and her, discovered, accused, tried, and hanged for witchcraft.

So she did nothing. Not because she didn't know what might help, but because she did. Because knowing meant danger, and danger could mean losing everything. And still, every cough, every ragged breath, made the weight of her silence nearly unbearable.

One night, when Benjamin had fallen asleep beside her with a scrap of his father's shirt clutched in his fist, she whispered to the darkness, "I will not lose him."

She wasn't sure which one she meant.

In her dreams, Elizabeth appeared again. She stood tall, fire licking at the hem of her dress, eyes sharp and unwavering.

"Know yourself," Elizabeth said, her voice steady. "Do not let their fear bind you."

Katherine woke with clenched fists, her chest tight, tears blurring her vision. Every doubt, every careful restraint, collapsed under the weight of that command.

She rose quietly and walked to the chest in the corner.

The key was already in the lock.

8

Broken

Katherine's hand turned the key in the lock.

She looked inside.

There it was, the book of fire, edges worn, cover darker than memory. It looked innocent now, almost humble. But it hummed. Even closed, it hummed.

Katherine reached for it. Her fingers brushed the leather spine.

And she stopped.

The room felt heavier suddenly, as if the walls leaned closer. She thought of the girl in the orchard. The question. The eyes. The whispers.

She slammed the lid shut.

The key she returned to the shelf.

John's cough worsened. What began as a rasp in the mornings turned into long, aching spells at night. He grew tired. Pale. But he smiled through it. Pretended it was nothing.

"It's just the damp air," he said, lips cracked.

She knew it wasn't.

Every day, her hands wanted to reach for the chest. To crush herbs. Boil tinctures. Whisper names of plants that healed. But she didn't. She couldn't. The colony watched too closely.

If John got better too quickly, too easily, there would be questions. And the town no longer asked questions to understand. Only to accuse.

So Katherine sat beside his bed.

She held his hand as it trembled.

She whispered stories to Benjamin in another room, pretending nothing was wrong.

She boiled soup and did all the things good wives did when their husbands needed it.

And John died.

Not with fear. Not in pain.

He held her hand, looked into her eyes, and said, "I love you for who you are. Don't ever forget that."

Then he was gone.

Katherine sat in the dark that night.

The chest still locked.

The key still waiting.

The fire still burning, inside her.

She had given the colony what it wanted.

And it had taken nearly everything.

But not her son. Not Benjamin.

Not yet.

9

Resolve

The fire in the hearth had long since died, but the air in Katherine's cottage still hung heavy with smoke, like it hadn't decided whether it was mourning or merely clinging to her out of habit.

She hadn't left the house in days.

The burial was quiet, unremarkable. No sermons, no psalms. Just a simple wooden cross over fresh soil and the breath of a woman who no longer feared judgment, because the worst had already come.

John was gone.

They said fever, but Katherine knew better. The sickness that killed him had been curable. But by then, the whispers in town had grown sharp, and she'd convinced herself to fold. To be still. To be the kind of woman they'd leave alone.

To still be a mother. To still be here for Benjamin.

She was devastated. Heartbroken. She mourned not only for him, but for the version of herself she had been forced to bury.

Now Benjamin lay in bed, coughing in that relentless rhythm. Small. Fragile. Skin burning with a heat Katherine didn't dare ignore.

She sat beside him, brushing sweat from his brow with shaking fingers. Each rasp of his breath made her chest tighten, the fear of losing him clawing at her. For a moment, she thought of staying still, of holding back as she had so many times before, protecting herself, her life, her future for the sake of the boy she loved. What was it worth to survive if he did not?

The book of fire. The one she had sworn never to touch. The one that could cost her everything. Katherine's hands trembled as she crossed the room. She told herself she was not acting out of defiance, but of love. That this was for Benjamin, and for no one else.

She opened it.

At dawn, she crept into the orchard, glancing over her shoulder at the cottages along the lane. A neighbor paused at her fence, muttering to herself, and Katherine froze, heart hammering, but the woman soon turned away, suspicious but not intervening. She moved swiftly, gathering the colts-foot leaves, stripping lung-wort stems with trembling precision.

Back inside, she brewed the herbs into a bitter, earthy tea. She fed it to Benjamin in small, careful sips, brushing his damp hair from his fevered forehead, whispering encouragement as she did. She stayed with him through the night, listening to his ragged breaths, her own fear mingling with hope.

By morning, Benjamin's fever had broken. He lay pale but steady, a fragile promise of life against the terror of the night.

But the whispers outside her cottage began again. Voices, low and cautious, circling rumors she could not ignore. Eyes would always be watching now.

10

A Knock at Dusk

It was three days later when they came. Dusk, the time of shadows.

Katherine answered the door expecting a constable with rope in his hand and judgment in his eyes. Instead, it was a man in a black cloak bearing the Governor's seal.

He didn't meet her gaze. "The Governor requests your presence," he said.

She stiffened. "Am I under arrest?"

"No, mistress. He… asks for your counsel."

That was stranger than any accusation. She had heard that the Governor had just returned from his voyage to secure the charter, and the thought of him summoning her personally made her chest tighten.

Governor Winthrop's estate stood at the edge of Wethersfield, its windows lit with the soft orange glow of candlelight.

She was led through a narrow side door and down a hallway that smelled of peat and herbs. At the end was a greenhouse, glass panes framed in dark wood, filled with the scent of dried lavender and chalk dust.

Winthrop stood beside a small table, sleeves rolled, cradling a boy in his arms.

The child, no older than Benjamin, was pale and soaked with fever. His body jerked with each cough.

Winthrop didn't look up when he said, "His name is Thomas."

Katherine froze. "Your son."

"Yes."

A tense silence fell between them.

"I've tried every tincture, every poultice," he said slowly, "nothing works. But… I heard of your son. How he recovered. How… people are saying it wasn't nature that healed him."

Katherine's breath caught. "You mean… they think…"

"They say it's witchcraft," Winthrop said bluntly. "I need your help."

She stepped forward slowly, eyes flicking to the glass jars on the shelves. Mercury. Valerian. Burnt sulfur. Vigils scratched into wax tablets. Colts-foot, lung-wort… the herbs she knew could heal. She blinked in disbelief. Everything she needed was here, at his fingertips. The Governor of the colony, the most powerful man in the land, with all the forbidden means and knowledge at his command, and yet he had come to her. How utterly hypocritical. How unthinkable.

"You're not just a Governor," she murmured.

He met her gaze, weary but unashamed. "No. I'm not."

She swallowed hard, looking at Thomas. The boy whimpered in fevered sleep, small hands trembling, fragile as a sparrow.

And something in her broke open. She stepped forward. "Bring me sulfur. Clean water. A sprig of yarrow if you have it. And the colts-foot and lung-wort."

Winthrop nodded once, sharp and urgent. He moved.

She did not speak the thought aloud, but it burned within her:

healing this child would mark her, and if anyone discovered it, suspicion could consume her. Every whispered word, every accusing glance could reach her.

35

But this time, she did not flinch. She had saved her son. She had acted, truly, as a mother. And in doing so, she felt herself whole again. What greater protection could there be than to save the Governor's child as she had saved her own?

11

The Heart Reclaimed

By midday, Thomas lay quiet in his bed, the harsh rasp of his cough softened into gentle, steady breaths. Katherine knelt beside him, brushing back damp hair from his fevered forehead, hands still trembling from the work of the night. Colts-foot, lung-wort, yarrow, and sulfur had done their work.

Winthrop, standing near the doorway, finally allowed himself a small exhale. "He is better," he said, voice quiet, almost in awe. "I feared… well, I feared my own knowledge would not suffice."

Katherine looked up, meeting his gaze. "You could have used every remedy in your estate, every experiment, and still… you came to me."

Winthrop shrugged, a wry smile touching his lips. "I have long loved the study of herbs, of remedies, of the natural philosophy. You might even call it my folly, but I know where my learning ends. And I have learned to value results over pride."

"You trust me," she said.

"I do," he replied, his tone serious. "But trust is a double-edged thing. What we do here, behind these walls, is not unknown. I can shield you in part, but the eyes of the town are sharper than any blade. They will not see your wisdom as I do. They will see it as danger."

Katherine's stomach twisted. "It is… maddening," she said, voice low. "You dabble in the very remedies, the very knowledge I risk my life for. You experiment, you collect, you study, yet the moment someone else uses them, the whole town cries witchcraft. The hypocrisy of it. How they fear what you secretly admire is unbearable."

Winthrop's expression darkened. "I know. It has always been so. I can indulge myself because of my station, my power. I can skirt suspicion. But you… you are exposed. And the town will not forgive what they do not understand. That is why you must be careful. Your courage cannot erase their fear."

She clenched her fists. "And yet, if I had not acted, the boy would have died. My son would have died. And what then? What is prudence if it costs lives?"

"Precisely," Winthrop said, softer now, almost reluctantly. "You have acted as a mother must. But remember this, your caution is not cowardice. It is survival. The line between knowledge and accusation is very thin."

Katherine absorbed his words, anger and resolve warring inside her. She had saved Thomas. She had saved her own child. And in doing so, she had reclaimed herself. But the world beyond these walls remained a place of dangerous superstition, where wisdom was twisted into accusation.

By evening, she had returned home, Benjamin asleep in the next room, and for a fleeting moment, she allowed herself to breathe.

The next morning, Katherine stepped into the market. Sunlight glinted off the wooden stalls, and the air smelled of fresh bread, dried herbs, and the tang of the river. She walked with a steadiness she had not known in months, her head held high, her movements deliberate.

Whispers followed her as she paused to examine the vegetables, to select apples for Benjamin's breakfast. Eyes lingered longer than necessary. Old neighbors, merchants, and mothers in the street murmured to each other, startled by the woman who had once shrunk from every gaze. She no longer flinched, no longer offered timid nods or downcast eyes. She was herself again.

A child dropped a basket of peas in surprise as she smiled down at him, helping him gather them. A woman at a spice stall blinked twice as Katherine asked about the dried mint with calm authority, her tone carrying the same quiet command she had once reserved for her own household. Some of the whispers were wary, others scandalized, yet Katherine met them with a serene gaze, letting them watch. As she turned to leave the market, a sharp voice cut after her:

"Don't think we're going to tolerate such pride in your step!"

Katherine paused, lips pressed into a thin line. Instead of answering, she looked up and noticed a flock of starlings spiraling high above the square, black wings flashing in the morning sun. A small, secret smile tugged at her lips.

She walked on, head high, carrying herself with the quiet certainty

That evening, she returned home with Benjamin, his small hand tucked into hers. She put him to bed, lingering at the doorway to watch him drift into dreams. Gratitude and love filled her chest. She had reclaimed herself.

She sank into her bed that night, the quiet of her cottage wrapping around her like a familiar shawl. For the first time in months, she felt the rhythm of her own life, steady and undiminished. She had defied fear, protected her son, and dared to be herself again.

Then came the knock.

12

The Cost of Courage

The knock was hard. Sharp. Certain.

Katherine froze. The words were not polite requests. The hands at her door carried neither reverence nor awe, only judgment.

And in that moment, she knew: the town had decided it was time to decide her fate.

The door swung open with a harsh creak. A tall constable, face set like stone, stepped inside, followed by another with a ledger clutched tightly under one arm. The morning sun fell across them in sharp angles, but it did nothing to soften the severity of their presence.

"Katherine Harrison," the first man said, voice loud enough to carry into every corner of the cottage, "you are under arrest for suspicion of witchcraft."

The words hit her like a physical blow. Her knees wobbled, her stomach pitched, and the world seemed to narrow into a tunnel of despair. The thought that had haunted her since Benjamin's birth, the worst possible consequence of her actions, had come true.

"No," she whispered, shaking her head. "No, this can't be. You can't take me. Not now. Not him.. Benjamin… please…" Her voice rose, cracking under the weight of terror. Tears streamed freely down her face. Her hands clutched at the doorway, at the air, at nothing, trying to hold onto a world that was slipping away.

The constables made no move to comfort her. One stepped forward, hand on her elbow. "We have our orders, Mistress Harrison. You will come with us."

Benjamin, roused by the shouting, emerged from his room in his nightclothes, rubbing his eyes. His small, worried voice called out, "Mother?"

Katherine dropped to her knees, scooping him up into her arms. "Shhh, shhh, it's alright, it's alright," she murmured, rocking him with desperate fervor. "I'm here, my love. I'm here." She held him close, comforting him with such fierce, unwavering devotion that she silently hoped the memory of it, the safety, the warmth, the love, would linger in his heart for the rest of his life, no matter what fate might claim her.

The men exchanged a glance. One, with rough hands and a stiff jaw, took the boy gently from her arms.

Katherine's scream tore from her throat, raw and unrestrained. "No! You don't understand! He's all I have left! Don't take him!" Her sobs rattled the walls.

The constables held her at arm's length as Benjamin was carried away, his small form disappearing into the courtyard. Katherine's cries followed him, echoing down the narrow streets, a sound so heart-wrenching it would have made the strongest heart ache.

She collapsed against the door-frame, trembling. The world had narrowed to a single, unbearable truth: she might never see her son again. The sacrifice, the courage, the risk, all of it had led to this moment.

Her sobs continued as the constables moved to bind her wrists, the weight of the unknown future pressing down like stone. Katherine's body shook, her heart fractured, yet in that raw, unimaginable fear, a single, unyielding spark of resolve glimmered, her love for Benjamin would outlast the terror of this moment, no matter what came next.

13

Accused

Katherine had been led through the quiet streets. Every face pressed close to the windows, every glance sharp with suspicion or curiosity. She was taken to a small, damp cell at the edge of the town hall. The first day passed in silence. She counted her breaths, tried to steady her racing heart, recalled every smile of Benjamin from the days before.

By the second day, a magistrate came for a preliminary examination. Questions came slowly, measured, probing her knowledge of herbs, her actions, her movements when gathering colts-foot and lung-wort. She answered cautiously, aware that any misstep could be fatal.

On the third day, she was escorted into the hall for the formal trial.

The hall in Wethersfield filled before the morning frost lifted. Every space was occupied. Standing, kneeling, even peering in through the windows from outside.

Katherine was led in by two men with grim mouths and nervous eyes. Her hands were bound with coarse rope, but her posture was unbent. She wore no bonnet, no shame, only a plain black dress and hair loosely tied back. Her eyes moved like storm clouds across the room. She met no one's gaze, yet made everyone feel exposed.

A clerk read the charges with grave urgency, as if racing time itself:

"Unnatural knowledge. Use of charms. Conversing with the dead. Familiarity with unnatural beasts. The brewing of tinctures unknown to any healer. Speaking words not of this world. Suspected familiarity with spirits. Attendance at unlawful gatherings."

The townsfolk didn't wait for instruction.

"She cured my sister's cough, then her teeth turned black!" shouted a man, red-faced.

"My cow wouldn't milk after Katherine walked past!" another hollered.

"She touched the water well and it froze that night!" cried an older woman, clutching her shawl like armor.

A neighbor alleged he had seen her drawing circles in the dirt and leaving pins near doorways, signs of curses, he said.

The room boiled over in noise. Accusations piled on like kindling: black crows gathering on rooftops, jars buried in gardens, the smell of sulfur, herbs too green for winter. One witness claimed she could make herself appear in two places at once.

Katherine remained still. Cold. Her expression didn't soften or break. When asked if she had anything to say in her defense, she rose. Her voice didn't tremble.

"What you fear is not evil. It is what you do not understand."

"You speak of dreams and weather and shadows as if they obey my will. Do you believe the wind listens to me?"

She turned slowly toward the crowd.

"I've cured fevers with willow bark and eased childbirth with ash leaf. You call that sorcery. I call it knowledge."

"You say my herbs are unnatural. But you boil roots for tea and call it medicine. You whisper charms when your children fall ill. But when I do it, it's witchcraft."

A hush fell, eerie and immediate.

"The specters you fear are of your own making. Yet still you hang ropes and claim it justice."

A woman dropped to her knees, weeping. A man muttered something under his breath and backed away toward the door.

But it wasn't enough. Not to cool the fire already lit.

A woman screamed from the gallery, her voice raw. "She cursed my child! My William couldn't walk right after she visited!"

"You speak of curses," she said, voice rising, cutting through the panic, "yet your own hands sow fear. Your minds twist kindness into sin. I have never wished harm. I only act with care. And now I am punished for the goodness you cannot understand."

The magistrates exchanged uneasy glances. Some shifted in their seats, quills scratching over ledgers that would mark her fate for history.

"Is it true," one asked sharply, "that you tend to the sick in secret, using herbs and incantations beyond the knowledge of any physician?"

"Yes," she said without hesitation. "I use herbs. I speak words of comfort. I do what I must to save life. You call it unnatural. I call it necessary."

A man bellowed, "She brought a fever to our town! My cattle fell ill, and my daughter's hair turned gray!"

"Is it my fault," Katherine shot back, "that illness exists? That life itself is frail? You speak of guilt and blame, yet you do not see the world as it is. You see only what frightens you."

The magistrates tried to restore order.

And then, a moment of silence. The court held its breath.

One magistrate leaned forward, gaze calculating. "Mistress Harrison, your courage is noted. But the law is bound to the testimony, to the fears of this town. You understand the peril of your position."

"I understand," she said, chin high. "I have acted as a mother. As a healer. I will not apologize for that."

Whispers surged again, louder now, a chorus of fear, suspicion, and awe. Some nodded at her words, others hissed. Yet Katherine stood, unwavering, the storm around her unable to reach the core of her resolve.

And in that storm, she realized something profound: even if the world would punish her, even if the ropes of superstition and fear were drawn tight around her life, she had saved her son. She had acted from love. And nothing could take that away.

The quill scratched on, the crowd waited, the magistrates deliberated. The verdict had yet to be spoken. But Katherine, for the first time in a lifetime of fear, felt the clarity of herself. She was unbroken. Whole.

The magistrates conferred quietly, noting each accusation carefully, as was recorded in the town records. The scribe kept writing, as if the scratching of his quill would keep the air from collapsing.

Finally, one of the magistrates cleared his throat, breaking the suffocating silence. "Katherine Harrison, the court has considered the charges, the testimonies, and the evidence presented. By the authority vested in us, you are found... guilty of the practice of witchcraft and unnatural arts."

A murmur rippled through the hall. Some gasped, some whispered prayers, some shook their heads in disbelief.

Katherine's posture did not waver. She met no one's eyes, and yet in her mind she held Benjamin close, the small warmth of his life a shield against the judgment around her.

"Your sentence is death by hanging. You are to be detained," the magistrate continued, "until further orders are given regarding your punishment and the care of your child."

The constables stepped forward, rough hands gripping her arms, and led her from the hall. Whispers followed, eyes lingered, but she did not flinch. She had been condemned by their fear, but she had saved Benjamin, and in that, she was whole.

The door closed behind her with a hollow echo, leaving the hall to its gossip and judgment. Outside, the wind carried the scent of frost and firewood, and somewhere beyond the walls, life continued: fragile, fleeting, and utterly human.

And so ended the trial, the verdict pronounced, the sentence declared. Yet Katherine Harrison, though bound and accused, carried within her the unassailable truth of a mother's love and a healer's courage.

The fate of a woman born into a world that expected her to kneel, and who refuses.

14

The Promise

Katherine sat on the floor, her wrists raw and swollen, rope burns stinging like open wounds. The chamber stank of damp stone and extinguished torches. The crowd's fury still rang in her ears, though the voices themselves had long since scattered into the night.

She would not cry. She would not give them that.

But silence had a weight of its own. It was the silence of something waiting.

Footsteps broke it.

Measured, deliberate, too steady to be a guard. Not the shuffle of fear, but the tread of someone who believed themselves untouchable.

The iron bolt slid back.

Katherine did not rise. She did not look up.

"You let them burn women alive," she said, her voice tight with fury. "You call it justice, while your hands are as guilty as any of ours."

A pause. Then a voice, calm, too controlled.

"Guilt," Winthrop said, "is not so easily measured in this place."

She lifted her eyes. He stood in the doorway, his cloak drawn close, the lamplight catching the pale angles of his face.

"You let Elizabeth Seager die," Katherine said, rising to her feet. "You let them hang her because it was easier than stopping them. Because you wanted the crowd fed. And now me. I save your son's life. Do you bury us one by one to keep their fear quiet?"

His expression flickered, something sharp passing beneath the calm.

"Do you truly believe everything you hear?"

Katherine faltered, just for a moment.

"And yet here you stand," he replied softly, "knowing how easily the eyes of men can be deceived. How willingly they believe what is set before them when it keeps order."

Her chest tightened. "Then what am I to believe of you? Of my fate?"

"Know this, Katherine: the noose is not always meant for the neck it shows. And I am not the man they think I am."

Silence stretched between them, taut as the rope she had feared at her own neck.

"Then why me?" she whispered. "Why stand here now, while the whole town would see me dead?"

Winthrop's gaze steadied on hers. "Because I cannot allow their fear to shape the only history we leave behind. You, of all people, must understand that."

She searched his face, desperate for clarity. But he gave her none.

"Trust me," he said simply.

Her laugh broke sharp, bitter. "Trust? You've hidden truths from us all while women choke on ropes in your streets."

He murmured. "...If you can keep your courage one day

longer..."

Winthrop's gaze did not waver. For a long moment he seemed to weigh something within himself, then he reached beneath his cloak.

When his hand emerged, it held a ring. A simple band of gold, heavy for its size, the surface scarred as though it had been hammered from raw ore rather than cast in a jeweler's mold. In the dim light, it glinted faintly, catching the fire like it held some secret within.

Katherine frowned. "A ring?"

His mouth curved, though not into a smile. "I call them the Governor's Rings. I give them to a soul that deserves sparing. A promise. A bond." He pressed it into her palm.

Her fingers closed around it, trembling. The metal was warmer than it should have been, as though it carried the memory of fire.

"And Benjamin?" she asked, voice breaking despite her resolve.

Winthrop's eyes softened. "He is safe. In good hands."

"Who has him?" she pressed, desperate for certainty.

He only shook his head. "A protector."

Katherine's throat tightened, but something inside her steadied at his words. If there was deceit in him, it did not reach his eyes.

"The shadows swallowed him as he moved to leave. 'You must endure, Katherine. Trust me. Hold fast.'"

The door shut softly, leaving her alone in the dark with the weight of the ring in her hand. She turned it once between her fingers, then slipped it onto her smallest finger. It hung loose, heavy.

And for the first time since the rope had seared her wrists, she felt the weight of choice settle upon her.

Not safety.

Not peace.

A small ring, dense and deliberate as if it were meant to purchase her trust.

15

The Gallows

The jail was quiet that morning.

Katherine sat on the floor, knees drawn in, fingers curled against her skirt. Much time had passed since Winthrop's visit, yet time had lost all meaning. Nothing made sense.

He was a man of government, of power. What if he lets them hang me to protect his secrets?

She pressed her forehead to her knees, gripping tightly. But the image of Benjamin wouldn't leave her. His small hands. His face when he was frightened but trying not to cry. His trust.

If they kill me... he'll think I left him. He'll think I chose this.

That thought alone nearly undid her.

I buried John. I will not bury Benjamin with my absence.

The door opened.

Two guards entered. Silent. One unfastened her chains. The other laid a folded black veil on the bench. No one looked at her.

She stood slowly, heartbeat thundering in her ears.

No one spoke.

She didn't move.

Then a voice, low and familiar, just above a whisper:

"Are you ready, Katherine?"

She didn't look. She reached down, picked up the veil, and let it fall over her head.

In the Square

The people of Wethersfield had gathered early. Even the wind seemed to wait. Mothers clutched shawls. Young boys squirmed with eager anticipation. Old men chewed silence like tobacco. They had come to witness a witch hang.

A veiled woman in black was led to the platform. Katherine's hands were bound, her pulse hammering. She did not resist. She did not speak. Each step felt both measured and unreal, as if she were walking through someone else's life. Courage surged, then ebbed. Trust flickered, then faltered. Her mind could not keep pace, fractured between fear, disbelief, and hollow, numb acceptance.

The executioner brought her to the noose. She teetered slightly, vertigo washing over her. She felt the rope's roughness, the platform beneath her feet, the weight of everyone's eyes.

And then… commotion. A distant rumble, growing louder, drawing eyes. The Governor's carriage, horses stamping, bells clinking, moving through the square like a storm unleashed. Mothers gasped. Children shrieked. The crowd's attention wavered.

Hidden hands reached for her. She felt herself lifted, shifted, guided into shadow, cradled in warmth. A whisper brushed her ear: "Trust."

She drew in a trembling breath, but did not look. The crowd below saw what they expected: the veiled woman, still and silent, standing on the scaffold.

The executioner pulled the lever. The body fell.

A collective exhale rolled through the square. Some wept. Some whispered. Some crossed themselves. They had seen what they needed to see: justice carried out, the witch punished, the colony's righteousness affirmed.

As the murmurs faded, Governor Winthrop ascended the scaffold, commanding silence. He surveyed the townsfolk, expression grave but resolute.

"People of Wethersfield," he began, voice carrying across the square, "you have witnessed today what we believed to be justice. Yet, I stand before you to declare that this marks the final execution of a witch in this colony. For too long, fear and superstition have guided our actions. We have condemned the innocent. No more. From this day forth, accusations of witchcraft shall be met with skepticism, not swift judgment. Justice will be tempered with reason. Let this be a lesson to us all."

Far from the square, the carriage wheels rattled over cobblestones. Katherine sat cradled against the cushions, heart hammering, mind still numb. Beside her, a man in dark wool shifted slightly, glancing at her with quiet assurance.

"You must be wondering," he said gently, voice low, "how it happened. The crowd... the scaffold..."

Katherine's fingers clenched the edge of her cloak.

"We arranged a substitution," he continued. "The body that fell... it belonged to someone already dead. A prisoner, unclaimed, a soul no one mourned. By the time the crowd saw it drop, they believed the punishment complete. It had to be convincing."

She drew in a shuddering breath, tears threatening, disbelief and relief mixing into a dizzying current. She had risked everything. Yet now, she had survived. She had been taken from the jaws of death, unseen and unclaimed.

Katherine closed her eyes, letting the weight of the words settle. Hope, fragile and fierce, took root. She had survived. And against impossible odds… vindicated.

The carriage rattled into the outskirts of Wethersfield. Silence filled the space between words, but the enormity of what had happened pressed into her bones. Her heart still raced. Her mind still spun.

And then she spoke, voice trembling but clear:

"Where is Benjamin?"

16

The Waiting Place

The inn stood low in Stamford, its windows lit with quiet flickering light. Benjamin sat beside the hearth, a wool cloak wrapped around his shoulders, his legs swinging from the bench. He gripped a mug of cider with both hands, too nervous to drink.

Across from him, a woman watched the fire. She was quiet, composed, her face kept mostly to the shadows. She hadn't said much since they left Wethersfield, only that she came "by way of Winthrop."

Benjamin wasn't sure who she was, but the name Winthrop was enough.

He glanced down at the woman's hand and noticed a small, shining ring on her finger. "What's that?" he asked, pointing.

She followed his gaze and held it up for him. "Ah. This?" She twirled it between her fingers. "It was a gift from Governor Winthrop himself. I had it etched with a little starling."

Benjamin frowned. "A starling?"

She smiled softly. "A bird. Small, quick… able to thrive in unexpected places. It's a reminder, for me, to watch out for those I care for. To trust, protect, and guide. And sometimes… it's a sign of hope. That even in a world full of danger, you can survive quietly, unnoticed."

Benjamin's eyes widened. "So… it's like you?"

Her lips quirked. "Something like that. But it's also for you, Benjamin. To remember that the smallest, simplest things can carry warnings, or guidance, or hope."

He studied the ring a moment longer, then gave a small nod, taking in the weight of her words in silence.

Outside, a quiet knock echoed from the back door.

The woman stood, gave Benjamin a look that wasn't quite a smile, and said, "Come on, boy. Someone's been waiting."

They stepped into the night.

Around the back of the inn, the fog thickened. She led him along a narrow path between two weather-worn sheds and out toward the tree line.

A figure stood waiting beside a wagon. Tall. Cloaked. Still.

Benjamin slowed. The woman beside him did not.

The figure did not move.

Benjamin stepped closer. His boots crunched the gravel softly. He could see the figure's hand now, pale, unmoving, resting lightly on the edge of the cloak.

The woman pulled back slightly, smiling through tears. "I never imagined… delivering a child twice would feel this way," she murmured, voice shaking with awe.

"Elizabeth!" Katherine's arms wrapped around Elizabeth as tightly as she could. Their breaths mingled, their hearts pounding in relief, grief, and joy all at once.

Benjamin's eyes widened, recognizing the familiar presence. Katherine loosened Elizabeth and knelt slightly, letting Benjamin see her face fully.

He stopped just a few feet away, staring up. And then, in a voice barely louder than breath:

"Mom?" Benjamin's small hands reached toward her. "Mom?" he repeated, voice trembling.

"Yes, my darling," Katherine breathed, pressing her palms against his cheeks. "It's me. I'm here."

17

Fate

History says Katherine Harrison left Wethersfield behind. She crossed into New York, carrying the weight of her name. A name stained by accusation, trial and conviction. But in that colony she left behind, something shifted.

Connecticut never hanged another witch. The frenzy ebbed. The courts grew cautious. And though whispers still clung to women who stood too tall, spoke too boldly, or knew too much, Katherine's trial marked the end of executions in that colony, decades before Salem would ignite with its own flames.

But what became of her?

No record tells. No grave bears her name.

Her death was never written, her resting place never found. The trail vanishes into silence, as if the world itself chose to protect her.

Her fate was not gallows or grave. It was survival. Untidy, unrecorded, unfinished. And that, perhaps, is why she still intrigues us. She slipped beyond the records, beyond the reach of those who condemned her, into a silence history could not close. A convicted witch who lived.

Afterword

Katherine Harrison was a real woman who lived in Wethers-field, Connecticut in the seventeenth century. A widow of means, she became one of the most infamous figures of the Connecticut witch trials. In 1669, she was accused of witchcraft on more than thirty separate counts. Her neighbors claimed she bewitched cattle, conjured storms, and spoke with the devil.

Her trial lasted nearly a year and divided the colony. Some demanded her execution, while others questioned the evidence and the use of spectral testimony. In the end, the General Court found her guilty but hesitated to enforce the death penalty. Instead, she was released on the condition that she leave Wethersfield forever. She fled to Westchester County, New York and there the records fall silent. No grave has ever been found. No document records her death.

Katherine Harrison is remembered today as the **last person convicted of witchcraft in Connecticut**. Her case helped bring an end to witch trials in the colony.

Elizabeth Seager, who appears in this story, was also a real woman accused of witchcraft in Wethersfield. She too faced multiple trials and was ultimately convicted in 1665, but never executed.

This is the statue of John Winthrop Jr., standing in New London, CT. More than just a figure in bronze, he played a pivotal role in the history behind Witch Fate. Winthrop Jr., governor of the Connecticut Colony, was known for his scientific curiosity, compassion, and skepticism toward witchcraft accusations. In a time when fear and superstition ruled, he stood apart, questioning the hysteria that ruined so many lives. His influence was key in bringing an end to the Connecticut witch trials.

What became of Katherine Harrison after she left Connecticut remains one of history's mysteries. She lived, though history cannot say for how long or how well. Perhaps that silence is part of her legacy: a woman branded a witch, who survived.

www.ingramcontent.com/pod-product-compliance
Lightning Source LLC
Chambersburg PA
CBHW050428110726
47899CB00008B/2891